PADDY'S PAY-DAY

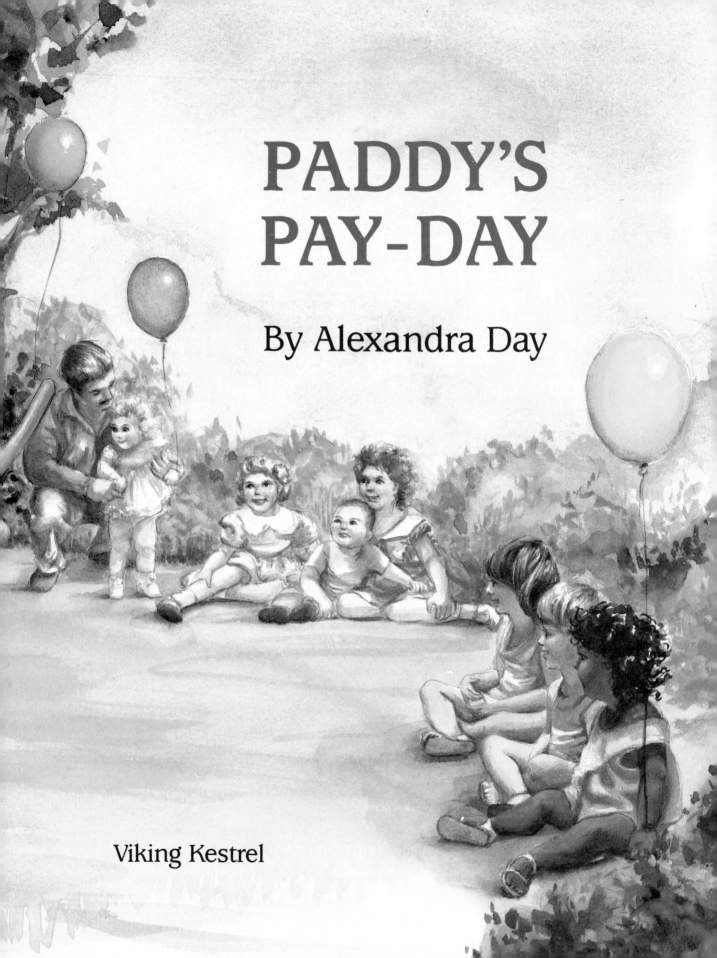

PADDY'S
PAY-DAY

By Alexandra Day

Viking Kestrel

VIKING KESTREL
Published by the Penguin Group
Viking Penguin Inc., 40 West 23rd Street, New York, New York 10010, U.S.A.
Penguin Books Ltd, 27 Wrights Lane, London W8 5TZ, England
Penguin Books Australia Ltd, Ringwood, Victoria, Australia
Penguin Books Canada Ltd, 2801 John Street, Markham, Ontario, Canada L3R 1B4
Penguin Books (N.Z.) Ltd, 182–190 Wairau Road, Auckland 10, New Zealand
Penguin Books Ltd, Registered Offices: Harmondsworth, Middlesex, England

First published in 1989 by Viking Penguin Inc.
Published simultaneously in Canada
10 9 8 7 6 5 4 3 2 1
Copyright © Alexandra Day, 1989
All rights reserved

Library of Congress Cataloging in Publication Data
Day, Alexandra.   Paddy's payday / by Alexandra Day.   p.   cm.
Summary: On his day off from the circus, Paddy, a performing Irish
terrier, spends a delightful day in a country town.
ISBN 0-670-82598-0   [1. Dogs—Fiction.   2. Circus—Fiction.]   I. Title.
PZ7.D32915Pad   1989   [E]—dc19 88-32236   CIP

Color Separations by Imago Ltd., Hong Kong
Manufactured through Imago Ltd., Hong Kong
Set in Usherwood Medium

FOR MY HUSBAND,
THE MYTH MAKER

"Here's your pay for this month, Paddy. Have a good time, but don't stay out too late."

"We don't have any Boston creams today, Paddy, but these strawberry ones are very nice. I've put your purse in your bag."

"Well, Paddy, time for
a trim again, I see."

"Your beard has certainly grown this month."

"You're right, Paddy.
Green does suit you best."

INEMA
CONTINUOUS
SHOWINGS
FROM 2:30
ELIZABETH TAYLOR ★ RODDY
IN "LASSIE COME HOM
ALSO SHOWIN
CARTOONS AND SHO
Now Playing
LASSIE
COME HOME

"Here's your ticket, Paddy.
Enjoy the show."

"So it's yourself is it, Paddy. I suppose you'll be wanting the usual."

"Here you are, Paddy; six roses and some heliotrope."

"Oh Paddy, thank you for the lovely flowers! I'm so glad you're home."